Apple Batter-Up

Dear Amelia
I hope you
enjoy this story!
Keep Reading 4
Fun.

Cheryl McNeil Fisher

Cheryl
May 2016

Dear Amelia

Nia 2016

Chapter One

Apples make delicious pies, but they also make for great fun. My sister Piper and I had the best time in the world with apples just the other day.

The day really began for the two of us that afternoon when Piper and I got dressed to go play outside. The sun was shining bright. We dressed in our long sleeves and jeans because it is the Fall season. I wore my pink long sleeve shirt and matching shoes. Sissy put on her purple long sleeve shirt and shoes. Sissy said, "Race you to the door." as she grinned and ran to the stairs. I started laughing and hollered, "Wait for me."

Just as we slid into the kitchen, Momma approached us from the dining room. "I'm going next door to check on Mrs. Mott. I shouldn't be gone long. Would you please take your baskets and fill them with apples from the trees on the side yard?" she asked.

"We really wanted to go play though..." I said with a frown.

"Kylie..." she said.

I looked up into my Momma's big brown eyes. "Yes?"

Momma crossed her arms as she kept her eyes fixated on me. "We are remembering to share responsibilities and what else?"

"Do everything without complaining or arguing?"

Momma smiled warmly as she nodded at me. "That's right, honey. When we work together, we get things done quicker."

She looked over to Piper. "Please peel the apples after you pick them. We will bake apple pies when I get home."

Piper nodded at Momma and said, "We'll pick them Momma. And would you tell Mrs. Mott that her dog, Buddy, misses her? He was lying around all afternoon yesterday! He wouldn't even play fetch!"

"He's an old dog, dear." Momma said. "I'll be sure to pass along the message to her. And Piper, you're doing a good thing, caring for Buddy while Mrs. Mott recovers from her twisted ankle."

Piper smiled at Momma and gave her a hug. I gave her one also before we skipped out the door. Momma waved to us before she gathered things to take next door.

Chapter Two

"C'mon, let's go stop by the barn to see Ruckus." Piper said.

"Okay." I replied.

The cool air nipped at our faces as we set our eyes on the barn across the yard. Piper turned to me.

"Race ya!" she exclaimed, as she darted for the barn.

"Wait for me! Wait for me!" I pleaded, chasing after her.

Piper likes to run. She is far too fast for me. I decided to walk and sing the rest of the way. As I came up to the barn, I saw Piper inside holding a silver stick in her hands.

"What is that?" I asked, as I approached to get a better look. The stick had rubber on both ends. One end was bigger than the other.

She began marching around the barn floor as she held the stick in one hand, shoving it into the air.

"I'm leading a marching band!" she shouted.

I walked over to say hello to Ruckus. I rubbed his velvety nose. Ruckus nuzzled my cheek. He knew I had a treat for him. I reached into my front pocket and pulled out a sugar cube. I put the cube in the center of my palm for Ruckus. I had to keep my hand flat, because he might accidentally nibble my fingers.

I looked over as Piper got down on her knees and put the stick under her armpit. "It could be a crutch for a small person." She paused as her eyes widened. "Or maybe it was for a child!" She gasped!

I gasped, "What child? It's only you and me, Piper! Momma didn't have any other kids."

She shrugged and said in a secretive voice. "Maybe it was for the secret society of pee-wee pony people!"

I was cracking up so much, that I was holding my stomach.

"Hey!" Momma shouted from behind us at the barn doors. Piper and I both whipped around at the sound of her voice. Piper dropped the stick so she wouldn't see it. "What are you doing with that baton?"

"Umm. Playing?" Piper replied.

Momma pointed to our baskets in the corner. "Weren't you going to pick apples?"

I said, "Momma, did you go next door already?"

Momma raised her eyebrow and said, "Kylie, are you trying to change the subject?"

I tilted my head and said, "Is it working?" Momma just kept looking at me with her raised eyebrow. I shrugged my shoulders. "Ooo-kay.", I said.

"I was just heading over to Mrs. Mott's, when I heard all that giggling going on." Momma smiled. "I'm going there right now. And, where are you girls going?"

We both shouted, "To pick apples!"

Momma shook her head and smiled, as she turned and headed back toward the path that would take her to Mrs. Mott's house.

Chapter Three

Piper and I made for the corner of the barn where we left our baskets. As we walked out the barn doors, I said to Piper, "Momma said that you are doing a good thing by watching Buddy. She is also doing a good deed by going over to help Mrs. Mott."

Piper nodded and looked over at me. "Momma says we are to help everyone we can. We need to treat others as we would like to be treated."

Piper grabbed my hand. "Let's go pick some apples." We skipped toward the apple trees in the side yard.

Looking up, I spotted the first shiny red apple I'd snag. With a grin on my face, I grabbed it from the low hanging branch. I turned to Piper, but she was already climbing up the tree.

"Good job! One down!" Piper declared.

We played while we picked apples. Piper swung upside down, handing me apples from the higher branches. We laugh so much when we are together. At one point, I was laughing so hard, I fell right on my bottom.

We sang some of our favorite songs, as we walked back to the house. We couldn't skip or run, because we might spill our baskets. After all, we worked so hard to pick all our apples

"Hey Buddy." Piper said as we climbed the porch steps.

Glancing over at the wooden swing, I saw Mrs. Mott's dog sleeping under it.

"How is he not cold out here?" I asked.

Piper said over her shoulder, "He's a dog. He has a coat on all the time!"

Chapter Four

As we came into the kitchen, we noticed Momma had already pulled out the pans for the pies and placed them on the counter. Momma also left two peelers, knives and a bowl for our apple peeling task. Placing the baskets on the kitchen table, we took our aprons off the hook, and slipped them over our heads.

Piper said, "We better get busy!"

I peeled the apples and Piper sliced them. One-by-one, each of the apples went into the bowl. That was, until about half way through.

Piper suddenly stopped and smiled over at me.

"What?" I asked.

"Remember the stick from the barn?" she asked.

I nodded slowly. "Yes. The thing Momma called a baton. What about it?"

"We should go get it."

"How come? We need to finish cutting these apples up before Momma gets home."

"It will be okay. She'll be gone for a while. Let's play a game."

"What kind of game?" I asked, setting my apple peeler down.

"Follow me," she replied as she headed out the back door.

I hastened my steps and followed after my sister. She led me back over to the barn and to the baton. Piper picked it up and tossed it between her hands. "This will do just fine!" she said with a grin.

"For what?" I asked. "Please just tell me!" I pleaded.

"The game. You'll see." She headed back out of the barn and I followed behind her.

As we bounced back into the house, Piper grabbed an apple from a basket on the table. She tossed it up a couple times in her hand. She smiled again. "The game is called... Whack-the-Apple," Piper said.

Chapter Five

"Whack-the-Apple? Like baseball?" I asked.

Piper scoffed. "No, no, no… This is no baseball, Sissy."

My eyebrows shot up encouraging her to continue.

"Whack-the-Apple doesn't have bases, or boring positions like left field and short stop. Instead, Whack-the-Apple is only hitting. You get points based on the splatter in the kitchen."

"Wow!" I shouted, jumping up and down in excitement. "Can I go first?"

Piper shook her head at me. "No… This needs to be tested. And since I'm the oldest,

I'll go first." Piper took the apple and baton over to the far end of the kitchen that connects into the dining room and said, "You must stand right here during your turn." Her eyes surveyed the kitchen as I made my way past her to get out of the way.

"What are you doing?" I asked from behind her.

She turned and said, "I'm setting up the point system in my mind right now... Let's see. On the counters, that's 10 points. On the walls or windows, that's 25, but if you manage to get the back door window with apple splatter, that's 100 points!"

I nodded. "Okay! Go!"

Piper lined her feet up in position and then tossed up the first apple. She swung the baton

around and missed the apple entirely. Her
face went red with embarrassment. "That
was a practice swing. Here goes the real
one!" she insisted.

Excitedly I said, "Swing batter-batter, swing."

She tossed another apple up and swung. This time the swing connected. As she smacked the apple with all her force, bits of the apple went in every direction, across the kitchen.

"Whoa!" I shouted. "That was awesome! My turn, my turn!"

"Wait!" she said. "We need to tally up my points. We need a pen and a piece of paper." She turned and ran through the dining room and up the stairs towards our bedroom. I followed behind her.

Chapter Six

We began searching our room for a pen and piece of paper. Piper popped her head up from near our bunk beds with my little pink notebook in hand. "How about this?" she asked.

That notebook was no notebook at all. It was a collection of my prized memories and experiences in life, many which included her. My heart about stopped as she held it up in the air.

"No! Give me that!" I demanded, as I snatched it from her hands. "Don't ever touch this, it's mine!"

She raised her hands up in defense as she stood and took a step back. "Sorry. I didn't know… it was just lying under your bed next to one of your dolls."

Holding onto the notebook as I held it up to my chest, I took a deep breath in and exhaled. "No, Sissy, I'm sorry… I shouldn't have yelled."

Something suddenly caught Piper's eye from across the room. "Why didn't I think of checking here first?" she asked herself out loud on her way over to the desk. Opening up a drawer, she retrieved a piece of paper and then snagged a pen from atop the desk. "There, now we can tally up points!" she said. She ran out the bedroom door and back down the stairs.

I turned around and went over to my bed. Lifting the corner of the mattress, I slid the notebook in. There, I thought to myself. It should be safe now.

Chapter Seven

Joining my sister back downstairs, I found her marking points as she walked through the kitchen. As I came in, she smiled over her shoulder at me and said, "You're going to have a hard time beating me, Sissy."

I began pulling my arm to stretch it and said, "I think I got this!" Piper laughed and walked back over to me.

"Okay, I scored a total of 60 points. Two wall splatters and some on the counter. Your turn!" I grabbed the Baton from the counter and hurried over to the kitchen entryway.

"Need this?" Piper asked, retrieving an apple from the table.

"Ha. That'd help," I replied smiling.

Piper tossed the apple through the air towards me and instead of catching it, I decided to swing. The apple exploded on impact and particles of apple went all over the kitchen and a bit of Piper too.

"Kylie!" Piper shouted at me as a chunk of apple fell out of her hair.

I snickered. "I couldn't help myself... you tossed it to me."

"Well... getting apple on me is not worth any points! So there!" She snapped. Turning around she glanced around the kitchen and marked down my points. "35 points. 10 for the counters, 25 for one wall."

I nodded. "Not bad..." as I watched Piper fetch another apple from the table.

She shrugged. "Yeah… in my hair." she said, grabbing the baton from my hand. I hurried behind her. My Sissy loves me, but I'm not taking a chance on her trying to get even. I heard her snicker to me, "Scared of a little apple?" We laughed. Then, Piper smashed another apple all over the place. This was so exciting.

When it was my turn again, we were both laughing so hard. I could hardly stand up.

I readied my position, tossed the apple up and swung... And the door opened at the same time.

~ SPLAT ~

Chapter Eight

It – was – Mamma.

Apple pieces shot across the kitchen.

Momma was covered in pieces of apple gook. One hand on her face and her mouth opened in horror. I think she clung on to the door handle so she wouldn't collapse. I don't know how long she stood there, but it sure felt like a very long time.

"Piper Lynn Makintosh. Kylie Ann Makintosh! What are you doing?"

Momma sounded as if she was growling like Buddy does sometimes in his sleep. And, umm, we knew we were in trouble because Momma said our full names.

The look in Momma's eyes wasn't one I had ever seen before. Never, in all the times Piper and I had been in mischief. She dropped her purse down on the counter next to the door and said very slowly, "Room. Now."

I set the baton down on the counter softly. We hung our heads and turned toward the stairs.

We were in our room for about ten minutes, when Piper looked over her shoulder and said, "Momma sure seems upset."

I nodded. "I know… I feel so bad."

Piper turned to me and said, "Let's go offer to help clean up."

"You think she'll be okay with that?" I asked. "I have never seen her so mad."

Piper nodded and took my hand. "She always helps other people, why can't we help her?"

"I want to help clean up too," I replied.

We made our way quietly down the stairs and stopped before entering the kitchen. Leaning against the corner wall that led into the kitchen, we listened.

Chapter Nine

The sound of huffing and scrubbing came from our Momma as she cleaned up our mess. Then suddenly silence. I was curious. What happened, so I glanced around the corner. She was lookimg up at the ceiling and asking, "Why God? Why me?" Momma was quiet. Then suddenly her face relaxed and, she smiled.

Piper was leaning over my shoulder, peeking into the kitchen with me. She whispered in my ear, "I think she was praying and God made her smile. She seems okay now. Let's go help."

As we walked into the kitchen, Momma stopped cleaning and turned to us. "I thought I told you girls to go to your room."

"You did, Momma." Piper began saying.

"But we want to help you clean," I said, finishing Piper's sentence.

Momma set her cloth down on the counter and crossed her arms but remained silent.

"We're really sorry about making a mess." Piper said. Then Momma broke out in a smile and said, "Thank you. I forgive you girls." She bent down and opened up her arms for us to hug her. Piper and I hurried over for the embrace. She kissed each one of our heads saying, "You two continually amaze me with your creativity. She began to laugh. Then we laughed. Before you knew it we were all laughing so hard that we had tears in our eyes.

"Let's finish cleaning up and then we'll start those pies." Momma said.

"Okay." we agreed. We cleaned the walls and everything in between.

Momma had to get the apple off the higher parts of the wall and even the ceiling. We were just about done when Momma went to her bedroom to change her clothes.

Piper went over to the pantry and pulled out the broom and dustpan. She did a quick sweep of the floor and I held the dustpan for her.

Momma came back into the kitchen, just as Piper was finishing her mopping. "Thank you for cleaning the floor, girls."

Piper said, "We wanted to do a good job helping you clean up, Momma. We're really sorry. Sometimes our fun, kind of, umm, gets carried away."

Momma laughed loudly. "You think?" "You girls keep me on my toes."

Chapter Ten

After we put the cleaning supplies away, Momma said, "You two work on peeling and cutting the rest of the apples. I'm going to work on making the pie crust."

When Momma put the pies into the oven, we all went into the living room. At the same time, all three of us collapsed onto the sofa.

Piper was on one side of the couch and I was on the other side, then Momma sat in the middle of us. I sat up and looked at Momma to find her fast asleep. Glancing over at Piper, as she sat up I asked in a whisper over Momma's chest, "You think she's sleeping?"

Piper shrugged. "She could be..." She leaned over Momma and began inspecting her face with her eyes. I watched as Piper pretended to thoroughly inspect Momma's face. Then I saw a smile begin to form at the corner of Momma's mouth.

"She's awake!" I exclaimed pointing at Momma's lips.

Momma laughed and sat up. Glancing over at the clock on the mantle, above the fireplace, she said "We have time for one book. I believe it is Kylie's turn to pick a book tonight, Piper."

"It is!" I said as I hopped off the couch and went to the bookshelf. Let's read Cindy Lou and Sammy's new book."

Piper said, "Oh that's great, Kylie." I always like hearing what Cindy and Sammy are up to next.

"We get to see and learn about different animals in this book." As I ran and leaped back onto the sofa, I handed the book to Momma.

Chapter Eleven

After reading our favorite book, Momma stood up and held out her hands. We each took a hand, and then Momma led us up the stairs.

We brushed our teeth and changed into our pajamas. We knelt by our bunk beds to pray.

Piper prayed, "Dear God, Thank you for this day. Thank you for our house and for our family and for our life. Help all the people that are sick in the world and that are sad. And thank you for an awesome little sister!"

My turn, I said. "Dear God. Thank you for this fun day. Thank you for my family and thank you for everything you give us. And thanks for my awesome sister."

Momma said, "Thank you for my beautiful girls and their adventurous spirits. Help us to keep learning and growing as we treat others as we would like them to treat us. We are also learning to help each other without complaining. Thank you again for Piper and Kylie."

"Amen." We all said together.

Sissy climbed up to her bunk bed. I snuggled into mine and waited for Momma's kisses. She first kissed Piper, and then leaned down to kiss me.

Before Momma turned out our light, she looked over her shoulder and said, "Sleep well my girls. I love you."

We both said, "Goodnight Momma. Love You too."

Shortly after Momma left the room, Piper hung down over the bed, giggling. "I love you, Kylie."

I smiled up at her and said, "I love you too Sissy."

"Sweet dreams." Piper said, as she swung back into her bed.   As I drifted off to slumber, I wondered what Piper would come up with next!

THE END *~ for now!*

Thank you for reading our story.
Many Thanks to my Mom for loving us
through our memorable escapades.
Love you Mom.
Thank you to both of my sisters
for creating fun memories.

GRAMMIE'S APPLE PIE

6 cups apple slices, (Grammie likes to mix two different types of apples. She says it tastes better.)
3/4 cup of sugar
2 tablespoons of flour
1 teaspoon of cinnamon
A dash of nutmeg
2 tablespoons of butter
Put apples in a large bowl. Combine all dry ingredients and pour over apples. Mix lightly. Line a 9 inch pie pan with crust and fill with apple mixture. Put a few drops of butter on top then add top crust. Crimp edges and poke top with fork so the can steam escape.
BAKE at 400 degrees for 50 minutes.
Cool and enjoy! Tastes real good with ice cream!

GRAMMIE'S BEST PIE CRUST

2 cups flour
1 teaspoon salt
2/3 cup Crisco shortening
5-7 tablespoons ice water
In a large bowl mix flour and salt. Use a pastry blender to cut shortening into flour. Work until dough is the size of peas. Make a well in the middle of the dough and add ice water a little at a time while mixing with a fork. Roll into a ball, cut it in half. On a floured surface roll dough with a rolling pin to the size you need. This makes enough for a two crust pie, like Grammie's Apple Pie.

Piper and Kylie's Baked Apples

This is our favorite because you can make it with one apple or a bunch. We'll tell you how to make it with 6 apples so you can share it with your family. Ask an adult to help you whenever you are using the stove and always remember to wear your oven mitts.

6 apples (peeled, cored and sliced) We like our Apple Peeler, Corer & Slicer. It's really fast. You need to use firm apples or apples that have been in the refrigerator. Soft apples won't work with peeler, slicer, and corer. They break up and get messy.

Spray a pan with cooking spray. We use the olive oil spray, but you can use the one you have at home. If you don't have spray, you can grease your pan or baking dish with butter.

Put your apples in the pan or baking dish.

Sprinkle with cinnamon sugar. You can get the cinnamon and sugar already mixed in a shaker.

Bake in the oven at 400 degrees for 30 minutes.

Spoon them into a dish while they are warm. Add ice cream and Wha-La! You have Yummy-in-Your-Tummy.

Momma told us we needed to put this in our story, so you wouldn't get in trouble. If you want to play Whack-the-Apple, ask your parents and play outside. Love Piper and Kylie.

ACKNOWLEDGEMENTS

Thank you Maureen Dwyer,
for your friendship, editing and recipes.

Thank you Jo-Ann Romanik,
for your friendship and editing.

Thank you Anika,
for helping this story become a reality.
Your illustrations capture the essence of
Piper and Kylie.

Thank you to all of you
for your support and patronage.
Piper and Kylie will see you again soon.

Believe in Dreams My Friends.
You Are Special.